MICKEY'S PERFECTO DAY!

Adapted by **Sherri Stoner** • Based on the episode written by **Ashley Mendoza**
Illustrated by **Loter, Inc.**

ABDOBOOKS.COM

Reinforced library bound edition published in 2020 by Spotlight, a division of ABDO, PO Box 398166, Minneapolis, Minnesota 55439. Spotlight produces high-quality reinforced library bound editions for schools and libraries. Published by agreement with Disney Press, an imprint of Disney Book Group.

Printed in the United States of America, North Mankato, Minnesota.
092019   012020

DISNEP PRESS
New York • Los Angeles

THIS BOOK CONTAINS
RECYCLED MATERIALS

Library of Congress Control Number: 2019943026

Publisher's Cataloging-in-Publication Data

Names: Stoner, Sherri; Mendoza, Ashley, authors. | Loter, Inc., illustrator.
Title: Mickey Mouse roadster racers: Mickey's perfecto day! / by Sherri Stoner, and Ashley Mendoza; illustrated by Loter, Inc.
Other title: Mickey's perfecto day!
Description: Minneapolis, Minnesota : Spotlight, 2020. | Series: World of reading level 1
Summary: Mickey and the Roadster Racers head to Madrid, Spain for fun, but a baby bull begins to chase them around town.
Identifiers: ISBN 9781532144035 (lib. bdg.)
Subjects: LCSH: Mickey and the roadster racers (Television program)--Juvenile fiction. | Mouse, Mickey (Fictitious character)--Juvenile fiction. | Mouse, Minnie (Fictitious character)--Juvenile fiction. | Bulls--Juvenile fiction. | Readers (Elementary)--Juvenile fiction. | Vacations--Juvenile fiction.
Classification: DDC [E]--dc23

Spotlight
A Division of ABDO
abdobooks.com

Mickey and his pals pack for a trip.
They are going to Madrid, Spain.
They will see the sights.
Donald will sing with his friends.
It will be a *perfecto* day!

The gang drives their Daily Drivers
to Madrid.

They pass a baby bull sniffing a rose.
The rose falls off the bush.
It lands in Minnie's car!

Minnie puts the rose behind her ear.
The baby bull runs after his rose.
Minnie does not notice.

The gang gets to Spain.
Mickey and Minnie go to the market.
It is a *perfecto* day!
The baby bull follows his nose to the rose.

Minnie shops.

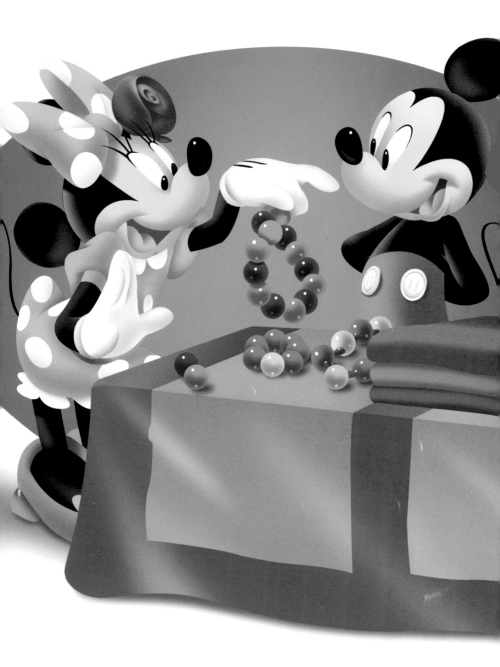

Minnie tries on dresses.
The baby bull sniffs the rose.
Minnie does not notice.

But Mickey notices!
"B-b-b-bull!" Mickey shouts.

Mickey and Minnie jump into a cart.
It rolls away from the bull.
It rolls into . . .

. . . a churro cart!
"We'll take two," says Mickey.

Donald finds his friends.
They invite Daisy and Donald to lunch.
It is a *perfecto* day!

Donald tries the potatoes.

"AAAACK!" he shouts.

They are very spicy.

Daisy tries to help.
She gives him water to drink.

It's almost time to sing.
The group warms up.
Donald opens his mouth.
No sound comes out.

Who will sing at the show?
Donald's friends ask Daisy to sing!

Donald is sad he can't sing with
his friends.
He gives Daisy his hat.

Poor Donald.

His friend brings him dessert.

He will watch the show from his table.

Mickey and Minnie visit the plaza.
The bull visits the plaza, too.

He follows his nose to the rose.
Mickey and Minnie run!

The friends find a spot to hide in.
The baby bull runs right by them.

Mickey and Minnie run to the show.
Daisy is singing with the band.

Donald finishes dessert.
He gets the bill.
"WHAT?" he shouts.
His voice is back!

Donald joins the band.
They sing together.
The crowd loves the show!

The baby bull comes to the show, too.
He sits next to Minnie.
He sniffs her rose.

"He just likes my flower!" Minnie says.
She gives the bull her rose.
The bull gives Mickey a kiss!

Minnie giggles.
What a *perfecto* day!